Don't Bug Me

by Margo Sorenson

To Jim, Jane, and Jill, who never said, "Don't bug me!"

M. S.

Cover Illustration: Greg Epkes

Inside Illustration: Michael A. Aspengren

Contents

1

The Bug Truck Pick-Up

Zack slid down in the front seat of the truck. How could his dad do this to him?

Zack hated first days of school. They were bad enough in September. But starting a new school in the middle of the year. That was the worst. He knew he'd be the only new kid. And, worst of all, his dad was driving him in the bug truck.

Dad stopped the truck for a red light. "Hey, Bobby! Lookit the giant ant on top of that truck!" The voice came from the car next to them.

Zack peeked over the window rim. Great. A car full of teenagers. They were all hanging out the window, pointing and laughing.

He felt his face turn red. Why couldn't he be invisible? He ducked back down and pretended to hunt for a pencil on the cab floor.

"Yeah! Lookit what it says on the side!" another voice yelled. " 'The Squish 'Em Squad! You Got 'Em, We Swat 'Em!' " Howls of laughter echoed in Zack's ears.

Why did his dad have to drive him to school in the bug truck? He had begged his dad to drive the old Ford. Anything was better than the bug truck.

"We're almost there, son," Bill said. He smiled at Zack.

Zack's stomach churned. He could see the school ahead. It squatted in the middle of the block. "Thomas Paine Middle School," read the marquee on the front lawn.

"Uh, Dad?" Zack asked quickly.

"Yes?" Bill replied.

"You don't have to drive me all the way to the front of the school," Zack answered. "You can drop me off here. If you want." He looked at his dad. "It'll save you time."

"No problem, Zack. It's on my way. My first call is in

6

the next block," his dad said.

Great, Zack thought. Just great. Now everyone at his new school would see him get out of the bright yellow truck. They'd never let him forget it. The "Bug Kid," they'd probably call him. Or worse.

Why did his dad have to start his own pest control business? And why did he have to drive a bright yellow truck with a giant ant on top? The ant even had a stupid grin on its face.

Why couldn't his dad have kept on working for his old boss? In that job, his dad drove a van with no bugs anywhere. Not on the top or the sides.

Zack saw groups of kids standing on the lawn. He was doomed. He knew it.

The truck pulled up at the curb. Kids stared. Some pointed. Others hooted. Laughter rolled out to meet him. He felt his face turn hot above his collar.

"Now have a good day," his dad said. "Work hard. Be proud you're a Washington."

Zack hopped out. He slammed the door. He kept his head down and walked quickly across the lawn. But voices followed him.

"Did you see *that?*"

" 'The Squish 'Em Squad!' "

"Who is that kid anyway?"

Their laughter rang out in the early spring air.

He opened the double doors of the school. They whooshed behind him. Safe. Well, for a while anyway.

The office was down the hall. His mom had taken him there Friday to sign up. Zack wished they hadn't moved just now. Couldn't they have waited until the end of the school year?

"Good morning," said the woman behind the counter. "Miss Hansey will be right with you."

Zack sat down on the edge of the chair. He waited for the counselor.

Zack sighed. He knew the reason they had moved now. It was all about the right timing. It was kind of complicated. But his dad had explained it to him when they first talked about moving.

"Why can't we stay here?" he had asked his dad. "I have my friends. I have football."

"Son, you know I can't start my new pest control business in the same town as my old boss," his dad had explained. "That wouldn't be right. We'd be competing." His dad shook his head. "He's taught me everything. It wouldn't be fair."

"Yeah, I guess," Zack had grumbled. "But why do we have to move in the middle of the school year?"

His dad had leaned back in his chair at the kitchen table. "It's like this, Zack. If I want customers, I need to advertise. So I advertised in the Yellow Pages. Without an ad in the phone book, no one would know to call us." His dad sipped his coffee. He looked at Zack. "No one would know 'Squish 'Em Squad' was even around. We wouldn't get any jobs. The business would never get off the ground."

Zack listened, his spirits sinking to his shoes. His dad had thought of everything—as usual—except for *him*. Zack sighed.

"As soon as the new phone book comes out, we'll move. With the ad, the business will be off and running, I hope," his dad had said.

So here they were. Right in the middle of the school year.

"Hello, Zack," Miss Hansey said. She smiled as she held out a slip of paper to him.

"Here are your classes. And here," she gave him another paper, "is a campus map. If you need any help, just ask someone. Everyone's helpful," she said.

Right, Zack said to himself. You bet. They'd be happy to help the Bug Kid.

"Your first class is science," said Miss Hansey. "Room 112. It's right down the hall. Have a nice day," she said.

"Thanks," Zack said. He got up slowly. When he opened the office door, a wave of sound hit him.

"Hey, that's *my* book!"

"Did you hear what Poppy said?"

"No way! They really did?"

Lockers slammed. Kids shoved through the halls, laughing and talking. Zack kept his head down while he walked. No one said hello to him. Why should they?

He sure wouldn't say anything first. That wasn't his style. Sometimes his parents told him he was too shy. But that's just the way he was.

Room 112. His heart beat a little faster. Here it was. His first class. Just as he reached for the door, two boys pushed past him. He bumped back against the lockers.

"Yeah, Sam!" one boy said to the other. "I can't believe you told her that!"

Sam tossed hair out of his eyes. "Of course," he said. He grinned. "Gotta be tough, you know." He laughed rudely.

They pushed past Zack into the classroom. Zack followed.

"Zack Washington," the balding teacher called. He held a sheet of paper. "You can sit over there." He pointed to the chair next to the guy called Sam and his friend.

Zack dropped his backpack on the floor. He slid into the chair. He waited for the teacher to begin class. Why did he have to be here? He hated this first day stuff.

"Hey!" Sam's voice broke into his thoughts. "Hey you. New guy!"

Zack turned. Sam was grinning at him. The other boy leaned across his desk.

"Aren't you the kid who got out of the bug truck today?" Sam asked, leering.

Zack's heart thudded. Oh, no. His nightmare was coming true. People had noticed the bug truck. Now he had a real problem. Worse than just the first day at a new school.

He took a deep breath. "Why?" he asked. He tried to

look casual. But his heart raced.

Sam hooted. "The Bug Boy!" he said. "The attack of the giant ants!" He thumped his fist on his desk and laughed.

The other boy snickered. He looked at Sam and the two of them cracked up even more. Then Sam turned back to Zack.

"Good thing you're in this science class," Sam said. "When old Mr. Barker tells us how small ants are, you can set him straight." He laughed again at his own joke. He elbowed the other boy. The other boy snickered.

Zack tightened his mouth. He turned away from them to face the front. There wasn't a bug joke he didn't know. He'd heard them all.

"Whatsa matter, Bug Boy?" Sam asked. "Are you bugged?" He cracked up again. "Get it, Andrew?" Sam asked his friend. "Are you *bugged?*"

The other boy choked with laughter.

Zack felt his face turn warm. At his old school, no one teased him about his dad's job. Back at his other school, he had friends. Good friends.

But then, his dad wasn't driving a bug truck either. A bright yellow truck with red letters on the side. "You Got 'Em, We Swat 'Em." Zack sighed.

How was he ever going to survive his new school? He'd never make any friends. No one wanted to be friends with Bug Boy.

2

Trapped

Zack thought science class would never end. In relief, Zack finally heard the bell ring. He couldn't wait to get away from Sam.

Three more classes passed in a blur. Luckily, Sam wasn't in any of them. Sam's friend, Andrew, wasn't either.

Lunch arrived. Zack dreaded it. He hadn't talked to anyone—except Sam and that jerk, Andrew. He hated eating alone. He couldn't help thinking of his old school. He and his buddies always had a great time at lunch.

Zack stood at the edge of the quad. Kids sat in bunches. They laughed and talked together. Where should he sit?

Zack frowned. He'd have to watch out. He didn't want to sit with losers by mistake. That would seal his fate for sure. That was another problem with being new.

There was a place. He walked over to a bench under a tree. Sitting down, he opened his lunch bag.

Voices called to each other. Chatter filled the air. Zack leaned back. He watched kids out of the corner of his eye.

Sure, he *could* talk to someone. He could start a conversation. But it was easier not to.

"Don't be so shy," his dad always said. But he wasn't really shy. He was just quiet.

Just two more classes. Then he was done for the day.

"Work hard," his dad had told him. Zack pressed his mouth into a thin line. Work was his dad's middle name. That was why he started his own business. No one could ever say Bill Washington wasn't ambitious.

Zack sighed. He knew he should be proud of his dad. But why did his dad have to be in the pest control business? There were so many other jobs!

How about a nice job running machines somewhere? Or a carpenter's job? How about driving a delivery truck? How about driving a forklift? Then Zack wouldn't be stuck riding to school in a bug truck. And no one would tell bug jokes.

RRRRINGGGG! Zack took a deep breath. Two more classes. Then he was done.

Not really, though, he told himself. He sighed. After school, he had to help his dad. That was something else new in his life.

"I can't pay a helper," his dad had told him last week. "Not yet. I need to get regular customers. Then I can hire someone. But until then, I need you."

Zack's heart had sunk. That meant he would have to ride around in the bug truck every afternoon.

He'd never have time to be with friends after school. He frowned. Not that he had any friends here. Like he'd even be able to *make* any. Not after kids saw him riding around in the bug truck.

But worst of all, he couldn't be in sports. He knew spring football would start in another three weeks. He had asked Miss Hansey about it when he signed up for school. But if he was helping his dad, he couldn't go out. Practice and games were after school.

Zack opened the door to his next class. Nothing was going right.

"Hey! It's Bug Boy!"

Zack heard Sam's voice. No. Not again.

A sea of faces turned and stared at him. Zack felt his face turn warm again. He gritted his teeth. His fists were clenched inside his pockets.

"You must be Zack Washington," the teacher said, walking over. She frowned over at Sam. Looking back at

Zack, she said, "I'm Mrs. Ames." She smiled.

Mrs. Ames showed Zack his seat. She handed him a textbook. He was happy to find he was across the room from Sam. Maybe Sam would leave him alone.

"Psssst!" a voice whispered from behind him.

Oh, no. Not more bug jokes, Zack thought. He turned around slowly. A kid was smiling at him.

"Don't let Sam get to ya," the boy said. "He's really okay. Kind of a jerk, but you'll figure him out. I'm Terry," he said. "I'm in your science class too."

Finally. Someone who seemed okay. He smiled at Terry. "Thanks," Zack said.

"Let's get started," Mrs. Ames said. "Please turn to page 165. Our short story is called 'If I Forget Thee, Oh Earth.' "

What a weird title, Zack thought. He turned back to face the front of the room. As he turned, he saw the girl sitting in the next row. She sat one desk ahead of him. Not bad, he thought.

He watched her turn and smile at the girl in front of him. Definitely not bad.

"Darla," Mrs. Ames said. "Would you please begin reading aloud?"

The girl began reading.

Darla. So that was her name.

He quickly turned to page 165 and followed along.

"When Marvin was ten years old," she read. Her voice went on for a few more paragraphs.

Mrs. Ames thanked Darla and called on someone else to read.

Uh-oh, Zack thought. His muscles tightened. He prayed Mrs. Ames wouldn't call on him to read aloud. He hated it. He wasn't good at reading aloud. He always stumbled over words.

Zack didn't mind facing a whole lineup of tackles on the football field. But read aloud in front of a whole class? Never! And what would Sam think of to say when he messed up?

The classroom got quiet. Zack blinked. Oh, no. Had he missed something? He'd been daydreaming again. What had he missed?

"So, what's going on?" Mrs. Ames asked. "What is happening in the story?"

A few kids raised their hands. Whew. Saved. He'd better listen.

Zack listened to what others said about the story. Some science fiction stuff. The people in the story were exiles from Earth. They couldn't live on Earth anymore.

Zack sighed. That was like him. He felt like an exile. He couldn't live here. All his friends were back in his old town.

At his old school, all the guys would be in math class right now. He thought about how much fun they'd be having. Willie'd be making spitwads when Old Turner wasn't looking. He'd throw them at the blackboard. When Old Turner turned to write on the board, little

16

sticky spitwads would cover it.

Zack grinned. Then he remembered where he was. He looked around quickly. Whew. No one saw him. Imagine smiling to himself. He wouldn't want Sam to get ahold of that.

"...and get into groups," Mrs. Ames was saying.

"You can be in my group," Terry said to Zack.

Groups? What were they doing? Well, he'd just follow along. He prayed he wouldn't have to say anything.

Students pulled and pushed their desks into circles. Darla turned her desk around. She pushed it into place next to Zack's. She smiled at him. "Hi," she said.

Zack choked. "H—hi," he stammered.

Terry pulled his desk up even with Zack's. Sam sauntered over. He dropped down into an empty desk. He grinned wickedly at Zack. "Hi, Bug Boy," he said. He looked at the others.

Darla and another girl frowned.

"Get a life," Terry sighed.

Everyone opened books and rustled papers.

"Hey!" A boy from another group leaned back in his chair toward Terry. In a low voice he asked, "Wanta go see *Swamp Babies* Saturday?"

"Yeah, sure," Terry said to him. "Call me."

Zack pretended not to hear. He studied his book. No one would be asking him. Besides, even if they did, he couldn't go. On weekends, he had to baby-sit his little sisters, Callie, Sallie, and Hannah. He had just found out last night.

His mom worked in a cafeteria downtown on Friday and Saturday nights. So Zack would have to stay home.

"But why can't *you* watch them?" Zack had asked his dad. "You always watched them before. You'll be home, right?"

"I need to be free in case I get an emergency pest control call," Bill told Zack. "I can't say, 'Sorry—call someone else.' I'll lose business. I need customers. It's a 24 hour-a-day job."

"What?" Zack had almost yelled. "I'll *never* get to do stuff with friends on the weekends?"

"Calm down, son," Bill had said. "This is just for a while. As soon as the business is up and running, I can hire someone else." He looked at Zack. "But until then, we need you."

Zack had slammed into his room. Fine, he thought. Just fine. Where was there room for him in this new life? I *am* bugged, he thought sarcastically.

"And what else? What can we add to the list?" Darla was saying. "What else could go wrong with the environment?"

"What do you think, Bug Boy?" Sam asked. He grinned meanly at Zack. "Or don't you know?"

Yeah, he had an *ant*-swer, Zack wanted to say. But no one would catch *him* making bug jokes. He wanted to forget everything about bugs. They were ruining his life.

3

Guess Whose House?

"What's the matter, Bug Boy?" Sam repeated. "Can't think of anything?"

Zack felt his face redden. He hated it when he had to say something. "Uh—uh, too much trash," he said.

Darla gave him a big smile. "Good idea," she said. She wrote the words on a sheet of paper in front of her.

"Bug Boy can talk!" Sam jeered. "He doesn't just wave his feelers."

Zack sighed. He had to pretend he didn't care. He decided not to say anything. Sometimes that was the best plan. Zack leaned back in his chair. He tried to look bored.

He'd love to get ahold of Sam on the football field. Zack hid a smile. Sam would be begging for mercy.

Zack was pretty sure Sam played. He'd heard Sam mention something about football to his friend, Andrew. Zack could destroy him during a couple of drills. No one would even notice—except Sam.

Then Zack frowned. He'd probably never get a chance. There'd be no football for him. He'd be helping his dad kill bugs instead. Zack slumped down a little in his desk.

"Oh, knock it off, Sam," Darla said. She smiled at Zack.

Zack gave her a small grin back. Darla was definitely all right.

"Class!" Mrs. Ames called out. "Quiet down, everyone. Let's share our lists." She waited for the class to stop talking.

"I need one person from each group to share," Mrs. Ames said. She looked right at Zack.

No! Please, no! he wanted to shout. His stomach knotted. He couldn't talk in front of a class. Especially all these new kids. Especially Sam—and Darla. Zack lowered his eyes. Maybe then Mrs. Ames wouldn't call on him.

"Um, Sam!" Mrs. Ames said. "Would you please read the list for your group."

Zack felt sweat break out on his forehead. Saved, he thought.

The rest of class passed by quickly. The bell rang.

"Hey, Zack," Terry called.

Zack stopped. "Yeah?" he asked.

"What's your last class?" Terry asked.

"P.E.," Zack said. Miss Hansey had put him in last period P.E. That way he could play spring football. Practice would start during class and finish after school. But now it didn't look like he would be playing.

"Oh, yeah?" Terry smiled. "Are you going out for spring football?"

Zack frowned. "Well, I'd like to. I used to play. At my old school. But I don't think I can here. I have a job after school for a while," he said.

Zack didn't want to say he was doing pest control. That was just too weird.

"You do? You're lucky," Terry said. "Wish I could get a job. I could use the money. Where do you work?" he asked.

Together, the two boys walked down the hall. They passed other students hurrying to class. Lockers slammed. Kids yelled to each other.

Here it comes, Zack thought. He took a breath.

"I—uh—I help my dad," he said.

Terry smiled. "Oh, yeah! The Squish 'Em Squad," he said.

Great. Now Terry would make fun of him too. Zack almost winced, waiting for Terry to say something. He looked sideways at Terry.

"Yeah, great, isn't it?" Zack muttered. He waited for the smart remark that Terry would be sure to make.

All of a sudden, Terry looked kind of strange. "That's cool that you can help your dad," Terry said slowly.

"I guess so," Zack answered, looking at Terry. "Well, not really. There are lots of things I'd rather do than work with my dad. Like play spring football," he said.

"Yeah," Terry said. "I guess."

Terry stared straight ahead. Zack wondered what was going on in Terry's head.

The two boys walked out into the sunshine. The gym lay ahead.

After class and his shower, Zack stuffed his P.E. clothes into his locker. The bell rang for the end of school.

"See ya," Terry called. He was tying his shoes. He grinned at Zack and waved.

Zack felt better. At least he'd made one friend today. He hurried out the double doors of the boys' locker room. His dad had asked him not to be late.

Wait. He was all turned around. Where was the front of the school?

Zack walked around the gym. There it was. He walked toward the marquee sign. His dad should be picking him up. So whoever hadn't seen the bug truck in the morning would be sure to see it in the afternoon. Super, he thought sarcastically.

Maybe he'd be lucky, and his mom would pick him up. Zack crossed his fingers. Then he could meet his dad wherever he was doing the pest job.

Please be on a call, Zack begged silently. But there it was. The bright yellow truck waited at the curb. Right in front of the school. On top, the ant's stupid grin beamed at him.

A knot of kids had formed around it. They laughed and joked. Zack could hear them all the way across the lawn.

"The ant! Check out the ant!" one boy said.

"Squish 'Em Squad!" a girl giggled.

Zack's face got hot. He wished the ground could open up. Then he could drop right in. But that wasn't going to happen. Zack took a deep breath. Here goes, he told himself.

Zack walked quickly up to the truck. Behind him, he heard muffled giggles and whispers. He grabbed the door handle. He hopped inside.

"Hi, son," his dad said. He smiled at him.

Zack turned his face away from the kids. That way, maybe they wouldn't remember what he looked like. He sighed. No chance. Who would forget a sight like this?

Zack's dad pulled away from the curb. "How was your first day at your new school?" he asked.

Fine, if you want to be called Bug Boy, Zack thought.

But aloud, he said, "Okay." He didn't want to make his dad feel bad. His dad was so proud of his new business.

"How was yours?" Zack asked.

"Pretty good," Bill answered. "The ad in the phone book is really working. I got nine calls today!"

"Great, Dad," Zack said. He brightened a little. Maybe there was hope. If the Squish 'Em Squad was really busy, then his dad would hire someone sooner.

"We're on our way to the last call now." His dad looked at the clipboard on the seat.

"Hall," he said. "A Mrs. Hall called. They're having ant problems."

Zack sighed. Ants. That meant they'd be spraying stuff.

Zack's dad had been doing pest control since Zack was born. And Zack knew more than he wanted about the pest business. Now he was even going to have to help. Was he really going to turn into Bug Boy? He imagined himself with giant feelers sprouting from his head. He shuddered.

"Here," his dad said. "This is for you."

Bill Washington reached behind the seat. He handed Zack a yellow shirt. It looked just like the one he had on. It said "Squish 'Em Squad" in small red letters on the front and in big red letters across the back. The giant ant grinned stupidly below the letters.

"Put this on. We need to look like a team." He smiled at Zack.

Now he really *was* Bug Boy. He slowly put on the shirt and buttoned it up over his T-shirt. He would just die if he saw anyone he knew while he was dressed like this. He'd have to keep his head down as much as he could while they were driving around. If his dad stopped at a store, no way was he going inside wearing the bug shirt.

Bill Washington pulled his truck into a driveway. The house was pretty big. It had two stories and lots of windows. It was sure different from their apartment. People who lived in houses like this must make lots of money.

His dad grabbed the clipboard. He opened the door of the truck and looked over at Zack.

"Come on! What are you waiting for?" he asked.

Together they walked up the path to the front door. His dad rang the bell. A woman answered the door.

"Yes?" she asked. She looked past them at the bright yellow truck in the driveway. She smiled. "Oh, yes," she said. "The pest control people."

"Mrs. Hall? Squish 'Em Squad," his dad said, smiling back at her. "I'm Bill Washington, the owner." He looked at Zack. "This is my helper—and son—Zack."

"Well, how nice that you can help your dad," the woman said.

Zack smiled weakly. Like he really wanted to, he thought.

"Come right in." Mrs. Hall led the way through the house. Zack noticed everything looked fresh and new. He sighed, thinking of their old, secondhand stuff. But at least they had stuff of their own.

Zack thought about Scott at his old school. He had wondered why Scott never had anyone over. Then one day, Zack found out. Scott lived in a homeless shelter. Scott would have been happy to have anything of his own, secondhand or not.

Mrs. Hall opened cupboards. They looked under the sink. She showed them where the ants had been crawling. Little black streams of ants crawled busily from around the pipes.

"Zack," his dad said. "Go on out to the truck and get the sprayer. Okay?" he asked. His dad bent down and checked the baseboards.

Zack found his way to the front door again. He opened the back of the truck and pulled out the sprayer. Slowly, he walked back up the path to the front door. Pink and white flowers and tall green trees framed the yard. The air outside smelled like flowers. The lawn was big and green. This was a nice place. He opened the front door and began walking back to the kitchen.

"Mom?" a girl's voice called. "Mom? I can't find my stapler." Footsteps hurried down the stairs. "Mom?"

The girl walked around the corner. Zack stood frozen in the hallway, holding the sprayer. It was Darla.

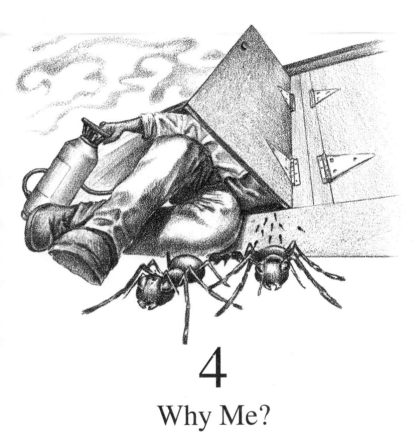

4
Why Me?

Zack's jaw dropped. He saw Darla stare at his bright yellow shirt. He flinched. He knew she couldn't miss the dumb ant printed above the pocket. Then Darla looked down at the sprayer. She looked puzzled.

How could this happen to him? Zack felt his face flush red above his yellow shirt collar. Of all the people to run into—Darla.

"Zack?" Darla asked. "That's your name, right?" But then she smiled. "What are *you* doing here?"

Zack's heart thudded. "I—I'm helping my dad," he stammered. His mouth felt dry.

"You mean about the ants?" she asked.

Zack nodded. He couldn't say anything.

"Oh," she said. She was still smiling. "That's nice," she added.

No way, Zack thought. It was the worst ever.

"How do you like Paine Middle School?" Darla asked. "Isn't it a pain?" she joked.

Zack smiled a little. "It's okay, I guess," he said. His hands felt sweaty.

"Well, gotta get to homework," she said. "It's a good thing you're gonna kill the ants. They give me the creeps."

She smiled and walked into the kitchen. Zack could hear her asking her mom about the stapler. He stood, rooted to the spot. He couldn't move.

Darla reappeared. "See ya," she said. Zack heard her footsteps going back up the stairs.

Great, he thought. He shook his head. Just great. What if Darla told everyone at school?

Sam would never leave him alone. Zack knew Sam would have all kinds of smart remarks.

"Why don't you come to my house?" Sam would yell. "I *termite*—I mean *might*—need your help. And wear that cool shirt. It matches the bug truck! You should wear it to school too—good advertising!"

Zack almost shuddered. Then he frowned. Wait. No. Darla wouldn't say anything. She wouldn't make a big deal out of it. He could already tell. She was pretty nice. He remembered what she'd done in English class. She wouldn't say anything mean on purpose. But then—she might say it by accident. He tightened his mouth.

"Zack?" Bill's voice called from the other room. His voice sounded muffled. He must have his head inside a cupboard, Zack thought.

"Where are you? Did you get lost?" Bill called again.

Zack took the sprayer into the kitchen. Bill crouched under the sink. He turned around when Zack walked in.

"What were you doing, son?" Bill asked.

Mrs. Hall looked at Zack. She smiled. "He was talking to Darla," she said to Bill. "You must go to school with Darla, right?" she asked.

Zack felt his face blush again. "Yes," he choked out.

"That's nice," Mrs. Hall said. "Well," she said to Bill. "I'll leave you to your work." She turned and left the kitchen.

"Did you meet her daughter today?" Bill asked. He began clearing things out of cupboards.

"Uh-huh," Zack mumbled. He couldn't believe it. Too much had happened in one day already.

At least they weren't at Sam's house. That would definitely be the worst. He could already see Sam following him around, chanting, "Bug Boy! Bug Boy!"

He'd never live that down at school!

They finished the job. As Zack packed up all their things, his dad wrote out the bill.

"Thanks," Mrs. Hall said. She handed him a check. "I'll call you again."

"Thank you," Bill said. "Tell your friends," he added, grinning. He handed her a bright yellow business card. There was the fiery red ant with the stupid grin.

"Of course," Mrs. Hall said. She smiled. "You can count on it."

Wonderful, Zack thought. Now all the Halls' friends would know that Darla went to school with the Bug Boy. They'd tell their kids. Pretty soon, there wouldn't be anyone left at Thomas Paine Middle School who wouldn't know Zack was the Bug Boy.

Zack sighed as they pulled into the carport behind their apartment. Why couldn't his dad be a checker in a grocery store? Or drive a truck?

Even before they opened the door to their apartment, Zack could hear the twins fighting.

"It's *my* turn to choose the channel!" six-year-old Callie yelled.

"It is *not!* It's *mine!*" her twin Sallie shouted back.

"Will you guys stop?" his eight-year-old sister Hannah yelled.

"Bill? Zack?" his mother's voice called.

She walked out of the tiny kitchen. She looked tired. But then, she always looked tired.

"Zack? Would you please watch the twins and Hannah for a few minutes?" his mother asked. "Your dad and I have an errand to run."

Zack tightened his mouth. He had just gotten home. He was tired. He had lousy homework to do. And now he had to baby-sit.

"Can't you take them with you?" he asked. He was just too worn out to baby-sit his screaming sisters.

"Zack!" Bill said sharply.

Zack hung his head. "Sorry. Sure, Mom," he said.

Well, he didn't really want to do his homework anyway. Especially that dumb story for English. What was the name of it? "I Can't Forget Earth"? Was that it? Zack frowned.

Zack went into his room and changed his shirt. He threw the bright yellow shirt on his bed. He didn't care if he ever saw it again. The ant just grinned at him from above the pocket. He shook his fist at it.

Grabbing his book, he walked back into the living room. The twins lay on the floor, their eyes glued to the TV. Hannah sat on the couch. She held her stuffed dog.

"...and so it was a good day, Raydeene," his dad said to his mom.

Raydeene smiled and brushed a lock of hair out of her eyes. She grabbed her purse from the table. Then his mother and father said good-bye. "We'll be right back," Zack's mom said.

"If I get a pest control call, please take a number. Tell

them I'll call right back," Zack's dad said.

Zack plopped down on the couch next to Hannah. Maybe, with any luck, his sisters would be quiet.

Hannah clicked the remote. The channel changed. A sports reporter was talking into a mike. He said something about the NFL draft.

Zack pressed his mouth together. NFL reminded him of spring football.

Zack looked over at the phone and hoped it would ring with more business. That was his only hope. With enough business, his dad could hire someone and he'd be off the hook.

Oh, no. Zack shut his eyes. He remembered what his dad had told him about answering the phone. He couldn't say "Hello" any more. Zack had strict instructions to answer the phone with "Squish 'Em Squad, may I help you?"

What would happen if his friends called? If he ever made any friends. He could just imagine what kids would say if they ever called him up for anything. He'd never live it down.

5

Wimps Don't Play Football!

Zack took a deep breath as he opened the door to his English class. Maybe he could slip in before Sam saw him and started yelling.

"It's Bug Boy!" Sam hooted. Too late, Zack thought.

Everyone turned around. Zack felt his face turn warm. Don't break, Zack told himself. Don't let Sam think he got to you. Pretend you don't care. Zack forced himself to walk cooly to his desk.

"Hi, Zack," Darla said, turning around in her desk. She smiled.

"Hey," Zack said. He tried to sound casual. He leaned back in his desk. Please don't let Darla say anything about yesterday. He almost held his breath. When she didn't say anything, he relaxed a little.

"All right, class," Mrs. Ames said. "You all finished reading the story last night?"

Some kids nodded their heads. Zack just sat there. Yeah, he'd read it. Callie and Sallie had been glued to the TV. So had Hannah. So he'd read the story. It was weird.

He knew it wouldn't be good to start out in a new school not doing homework. He might slack a little later. But not at the beginning anyway.

"Who would like to summarize the story?" Mrs. Ames asked. She looked at the class.

Zack slid down in his seat. No way was he going to get called on. He knew how to keep teachers from calling on him. He had to look a little interested, but not too much.

It usually worked. Good thing, because he hated to speak up in class. He'd rather die.

Zack looked at the other students. Some kid across the room raised a hand. Great, Zack thought. A volunteer.

"The story is about a human colony on another planet. A kid learns that humans had to leave Earth. Earth was wrecked or something."

Mrs. Ames smiled. "Thank you, Verna." She looked

around the room. "Can someone else add to what Verna said? How was the earth 'wrecked'? What message is the author giving us?"

Some other kid raised a hand. Whew, Zack thought. Good thing *somebody* wanted to talk in class.

"I think it was some nuclear bomb or something," the boy said. "And the author is trying to tell us that we have to take care of our planet. I think," he said.

Yeah, Zack decided. That's what he thought. At least he wasn't too far off.

"We do have to take care of the Earth," Mrs. Ames said. "Nicely said, Carl and Verna." She picked up a colored marker and walked to the board.

"We're going to do group projects," she said, turning around. "There are many ideas in the story. First, your group will talk about the story together."

She began writing on the board. She numbered the steps.

"You'll share ideas. Then you'll decide what you want to show the class. Your group will act out or present an idea to the class about the story."

She finished writing. She turned and smiled at the class.

Zack felt his stomach flip. No way was *he* going to stand up in front of the class. He'd have to stay home from school that day. This new school was going to be tough.

"Any questions?" Mrs. Ames asked.

Darla raised her hand.

"Yes, Darla?" Mrs. Ames said.

"How long do we have to work on it?" Darla asked. "I mean, before we have to share?"

"You have two weeks," Mrs. Ames said. "We'll start presentations a week from next Monday."

Mrs. Ames suddenly looked at Zack. She looked thoughtful.

"Zack?" she said.

Zack's heart thudded. He could feel everyone's eyes on him. Oh no. What was it?

"Y—Yes?" he stammered. He felt his forehead bead up with sweat. What was Mrs. Ames going to do? Was he in trouble already? Did he have to say something about the story? Did he have to talk in front of the whole class?

"You can be in the same group you were in yesterday," Mrs. Ames said. "With Terry and Darla."

"Okay," Zack mumbled. A wave of relief washed over him. Whew, he thought. Saved again.

Out of the corner of his eye, Zack saw Terry give him a thumbs-up and a grin. It was nice to have a friend.

And Darla was in the group too. But so was Sam. Zack frowned.

Then Zack flinched. What if Darla said something about the pest control call yesterday? Sam would hear. Then he would make fun of Zack again.

Zack pressed his lips into a thin line. He'd figure out a way to get at Sam. If only he could crush him on the football practice field. Nobody would even think twice. In football you could do stuff like that. Then it was okay.

Zack tapped his fingers on his desk. He wasn't going to put up with this junk much longer. Even if he *didn't* play football, he'd get Sam somehow.

Desks clattered. Students pulled them into circles to work with their groups. Zack pulled his desk next to Terry.

"Hey, man," Terry said. "Same group. Good deal, right?" He grinned.

"Yeah," Zack agreed. Terry was turning out to be a good friend.

"So, Bug Boy, whaddaya think about the story?" Sam asked rudely.

Zack couldn't think of anything to say. His tongue felt tied.

"Be quiet, Sam," Darla said. She sat down. She looked at Sam. "Since you're so enthusiastic, why don't *you* start?"

Sam made a face. "Actually," he said, "I didn't finish the dumb story. I thought it was lame."

Hah! Zack thought. So much for you, big mouth.

Darla sighed. "Good work, Sam," she said sarcastically. "Thanks for the help." She looked at another student. "Jenaya, what did you think?"

Jenaya leaned forward. "Well," she said, "I liked the story. I liked how it showed how bad things could get."

"I thought so too," Darla said. "What did you think, Zack?"

Zack felt his face get hot. "I—I—uh liked it too," he mumbled.

Terry broke in. Zack was saved again.

"I think we oughta do something about how the Earth will be a disaster soon," Terry said. He tapped his pencil on his desk. His feet twisted and untwisted around the desk legs.

"Yeah, we could," Darla agreed. She looked at everyone. "So what should we do? Any ideas?" She stared at Sam. "Sam?" she asked. She tapped her pencil on her notebook.

Sam slid down in his desk. "I dunno," he said. "Let's show a bunch of fighting and stuff."

"That's weak," Jenaya said. She looked at Sam. "There are lots of other things more important than that." She made a face.

"Like the Earth getting too hot?" Terry asked. He leaned forward in his desk. "We're learning about that in science, right?" He looked at Zack.

Uh-oh, was he going to have to say something now? Zack wondered. His mouth felt dry. "Uh-huh," he choked out.

"Global warming," Darla said. "We could show how hot things are." She wrote on the sheet of paper on her desk. She erased something and blew the dust off the page.

"We could pretend to fry an egg on the floor," Jenaya chimed in. Her eyes twinkled. She jiggled an imaginary frying pan over a fire.

"We gotta do something good," Sam complained. "I'm getting a *D* in this class. I'm not gonna be able to play football if I don't bring up my grade."

"We'd all like to get a decent grade," Darla said. "Okay. Frying an egg." She stopped. "I don't know how we can do that. Maybe we'll think of something. What else can we do? What else can go wrong?"

Zack knew one big problem was chemicals. People could use too many chemicals. They could use them in the wrong way. Then bugs wouldn't die from them any more. The bugs would be immune. Soon, there would be giant bugs crawling the earth. He sure wasn't going to bring *that* up, though. He could just hear what Sam would say.

So Zack sat quietly. Let everyone else give ideas. He'd stay in the background. He wasn't going to say anything in front of anyone. And definitely not in front of the whole class.

The conversation went on. Finally, the bell rang. Mrs. Ames dismissed the class.

Zack and Terry hurried to P.E. They rushed through the double doors of the locker room. Suddenly, Zack felt a hand on his shoulder. He froze.

"Zack Washington, right?" a deep voice asked.

Zack turned around to see Coach Dunwoody, his P.E. teacher. He was smiling.

"Uh—uh, yeah," he mumbled.

"I was watching you yesterday in class. You've got a lot of speed." Coach folded his arms. He rocked back on his heels. "Have you thought about going out for spring football?"

Zack looked down at the ground. "Uh, yeah," he said. "I got scheduled in this period so maybe I could." He looked up at the coach. "But now my dad says I can't. I have to help him at his job after school."

Coach looked disappointed. "That's too bad," he said. "Is there any chance that might change?" he asked.

"Maybe," Zack said. "I'll let you know."

"Do that," Coach Dunwoody said. "Now get changed for class, you slacker," he joked.

Zack began to hustle down the rows of lockers.

"Hey, Bug Boy," Sam called to him from the end of the row. "Coach tell you that you were too wimpy to go out for football?" he leered. "Bug Boy can't play football? You could take your bug spray out onto the field. You could spray those linemen!"

Zack felt blood rush angrily to his head. Sam just never stopped!

6

I Can't Go

"Dad, please?" Zack begged. He put his spoon down in his cereal bowl.

It was Saturday morning. The family sat around the tiny table. Callie and Sallie shoveled cereal into their mouths. Hannah gulped her milk.

"Please?" Zack repeated. "I'll work for you every *other* day. I promise."

"Zack, I'm sorry. I really am. But I need your help." He drank some coffee from his mug.

"Can't you hire another guy really soon just in case it does get busy? You've already gotten lots of calls, right?" Zack asked. "The phone rings all the time." He stirred the cereal in his bowl faster and faster. "I gotta go out for football. I just gotta." He looked at his dad.

Zack loved football. Plus, he knew football would help get rid of the Bug Boy image.

Bill slammed down his coffee cup. Callie's and Sallie's eyes opened wide. Hannah stared.

Zack's stomach flipped. Great. Now he'd made his dad mad. You idiot, he told himself.

"When I say no, I mean *no,*" Bill said firmly. He looked at Zack. He pressed his mouth into a thin line. Then he sighed.

"I know, son. Football means a lot to you," his dad said, more calmly. "I'd love to see you play. And, yes, I'd like to hire someone now too. But I just can't yet.

"We'll work hard to make money," Bill continued. "I promise. We'll be a team." He sipped his coffee. "Who knows? I might be able to pay someone sooner than we think. You never know." He put his coffee mug down.

Zack's face felt hot. He did *not* want to be a bug team with his dad. The only team he was interested in was the football team. But if working hard is what it took, he'd gut it out.

"Yeah, Dad. I'm sorry," he mumbled, red-faced. He stared down at the soggy flakes in his cereal bowl.

"Your dad and I work hard," Raydeene said. "And we

all have to make some sacrifices. We need your cooperation, Zack," she added. "That goes for baby-sitting too."

"Yes, Mom," Zack said. Wonderful. Here he was starting out the weekend with a lecture again. Why was it so tough being a kid? All he wanted was to have a life like other kids. He didn't want to be a Bug Boy. That was no life at all. Parents just didn't get it.

Early that afternoon, his mother left to work at the cafeteria. Zack could hear the old Ford chug-chugging down the street. That was another thing. They needed a new car too. The Ford was just about dead, his dad said. Just one more reason for his dad not to hire someone. He groaned at the thought.

"Zack, Callie has my Rock-a-Bye Pony!" Sallie screamed. She tugged at one end of a bright pink, stuffed pony.

"Nuh-uh! It's not yours! It's *mine!*" Callie screamed back. She tugged on the other end of the pony.

"Zack, will you make them shut up?" Hannah yelled. "I can't hear the TV!" She turned around and glared at him.

Zack sighed. Great. His mom had just left, and his sisters were already a pain. He'd almost rather be at school. At least at school, no baby sisters could bug him.

Hah! he thought. Maybe he could just borrow his dad's sprayer and zap his pesty sisters, once and for all.

"Zack?" his dad called. "I'm leaving for the

Matthews' job. The phone number is on the message pad. Watch the girls closely."

"Sure, Dad," Zack groaned.

Now his dad wouldn't be around to answer the phone. It would be up to him. He'd already answered it a few times with "Squish 'Em Squad. May I help you?"

Just this morning, a lady on the other end of the line had giggled after he said it. Zack could feel his face turn red. He was so embarrassed that he had trouble talking after that. Well, at least the phone was really ringing a lot with customers. That was a good sign.

Callie and Sallie were still grunting as they tugged at the ends of the pink pony. He heard his dad shut the door behind him.

"All right, you two," Zack growled. "Playtime is *over!*" He got up from the couch.

BUZZZZ! The front door buzzed. Had Dad forgotten something? Why couldn't he open the door himself?

Zack walked to the door. He opened it.

"Hey, man," said Terry, grinning.

"Terry!" Zack said. He smiled back. "What're you doing here?"

"Can I come in? Or do I have to stay out in the hall?" Terry asked, still grinning.

"Oh—uh, yeah! Sorry!" Zack stumbled. He wasn't used to having anyone stop by since he'd moved. He really didn't know anyone. Besides, who would come to visit Bug Boy?

"You told me you might be home this afternoon," Terry explained. He held up some black rollerblades with fluorescent green blades. "So I thought I'd come by and see if you want to go rollerblading. My cousin just gave me his old ones."

Zack held back a sigh. "I don't have rollerblades," he said. And probably never would, at least not for a while, he added silently. "Otherwise, I'd love to go. Hey, thanks for asking anyway." He looked down at the ground.

Terry looked disappointed. He dropped his arm. The rollerblades dangled from his hand by their laces.

"So, how about heading over to the mall?" Terry asked. "I can show you where stuff is," he said. "We could meet up with Ross and Brandon. They're gonna be there."

Zack frowned. This was getting worse. He looked over at Sallie and Callie. Callie had grabbed the pink pony away from Sallie. Now she was hugging it and sticking her tongue out at Sallie.

Sallie was kicking at Callie with her feet, saying, "Mine! It's mine!"

"Shut *up!*" Hannah said without looking away from the blaring TV set. She lay on her stomach, kicking her feet together in the air. She was watching a rerun Zack knew she had seen at least a million times!

Zack gestured at the three girls. He looked at Terry. Zack made a face.

"This is my job this afternoon and tonight. And

Sunday too. I don't have a life." He sighed. "I can't go anywhere on the weekend," Zack added. "Until my dad can hire someone."

Zack walked over to the couch and dropped down on it. Terry followed.

"Who's *that?*" Callie asked.

At least the twins had stopped their fighting long enough to stare at Terry. Hannah turned around and stared too.

Terry grinned. "I'm Terry. Who're you?" he asked the girls.

Zack was thrilled to actually have a friend over. At his old apartment, his buddies were always stopping by. Sometimes there were more friends than there were Washingtons in the place. But he didn't think Bug Boy would ever have that many friends.

"So how come you're baby-sitting all the time?" Terry asked Zack. "You work after school too, don't you?"

"Well, my dad needs me a lot," Zack sighed. "Until he can get his business going."

"Oh, yeah?" Terry said slowly. He stopped. He stared at the TV for a minute. Then he turned to look at Zack. "It—it must be kinda nice that your dad needs you," he said quietly.

What does he mean? Zack wondered. He looked at Terry's face, trying to read it.

"Why do you say that?" Zack asked Terry. "I'd rather

be with my friends than my dad," he complained.

"Yeah? Well, I don't even have a dad," Terry said shortly.

Zack felt his face blush. Great. Just great. Terry had no dad. And here he was complaining about his. He had put his foot in his mouth again. And with his new friend too.

Zack couldn't think of anything to say. Besides, he'd probably say the wrong thing anyway. Then he'd just get himself in trouble again. "Sorry" would just sound lame.

But then Terry lifted his chin. "So, when do you think you'll get out of this prison?" he joked.

Zack felt relief wash over him. Maybe things would be all right. Terry was okay. He didn't seem mad.

"Uh—uh—if my dad can hire a guy. Then the guy can work during the week instead of me. And take calls for my dad on the weekends," Zack said. "Right now, my dad has to do everything. So I have to help him *and* baby-sit."

"Leave me *alone!*" Hannah suddenly yelled. "I can't *see!*"

Callie and Sallie were hopping their ponies over Hannah's legs. Hannah pushed and elbowed the two younger girls.

"Oweeee! Oweeee!" Callie sobbed. Big tears rolled down her chubby cheeks.

"Zack! Hannah hurt me!" Sallie yelled. She rubbed her stomach.

Terry grinned at Zack. "Well, looks like you're plenty busy. Too bad I can't stay and help out," he joked. "But I told Brandon and Ross I'd probably see them. Sorry you can't go," he added.

Terry stood up to go. Zack got to his feet too.

"Uh, me too," Zack said. He sighed. "But thanks for stopping over."

"Sure. No problem," Terry said. He walked to the door.

"Come any time," Zack said. He stopped. He'd never be home except on the weekends. "On the weekends, I mean," he added.

"Sal*lllieeee!*" Hannah yelled.

Thumps and bumps came from behind the couch.

"I said *stop it!*" Hannah shouted. "Zack! They're ganging up on me!"

Terry looked over at the three girls fighting. He grinned lopsidedly.

"Yeah, sure, next time I'll stay and help baby-sit," he joked. "See ya," he said. He walked through the door.

Zack shut the door. Well, that was probably the last time Terry would want to come over. He frowned.

See? he wanted to yell at his sisters. See what you've done? No one will ever want to come over here, and it's all because of you! He fumed silently at his sisters.

No friends. No football. No life. Not for Bug Boy.

He felt squashed. He might as well be just a plain old bug for all the fun he was having.

7

EEEEEEEEK!

"All right, class," Mrs. Ames said Monday afternoon. She rapped a pencil on her desk.

Kids began to settle down. Zack watched his classmates as he thought about earlier that morning.

His dad had driven him to school, as usual. When he got out of the bug truck, kids still grinned and whispered. But at least no one laughed out loud.

By now, Zack was sure everyone at Thomas Paine Middle School knew who he was. Sam had seen to that. Zack thought he might as well pull the giant ant behind him on a leash to all his classes. He might as well wear his bright yellow shirt to school. He shuddered. Well, at least today Sam hadn't yelled out, "Bug Boy's here!" when Zack walked into English class.

Also, Zack had met Terry for lunch. Brandon and Ross were there too. It had been fun. Maybe the scene with his sisters hadn't been so bad after all.

"...so some of your groups will meet in the core area," Mrs Ames said. She looked at the class.

Oh no, Zack thought. He'd zoned out again just when Mrs. Ames was giving directions. He had to start paying closer attention.

Zack looked at Darla. She was busy taking notes. Zack was glad someone was paying attention. Darla would know what to do.

"Darla, your group can meet in the core area," Mrs. Ames said. "Okay, class. Let's get to work."

Zack wondered about the core area. It sounded like the inside of an apple. Slowly, he got up. He took his book and a notebook and followed Darla and Terry.

"Hey, man, let's go," Terry called to him, grinning. He nodded his head toward some windows on the classroom wall.

Miniblinds covered the windows, so Zack couldn't see inside. He had noticed a door in the wall of windows.

He thought it led to another classroom. Darla opened it. Terry, Sam, Jenaya, and Zack followed her. Zack looked around. It was like another classroom, except it looked like an office.

Teachers' desks sat in every corner. Through the windows, he could see into other classrooms. The core was in the middle of the building. Cupboards lined some of the walls under the windows. Books were stacked on shelves.

Darla plopped down on the carpet. Jenaya sat next to her. Zack thought how he'd like to sit next to Darla too. His face felt warm.

Zack dropped down opposite Darla. Terry sat down, and Sam stretched out on his stomach.

"Aaaah, nap time," he said, closing his eyes. "Keep the bugs off me, will you, Bug Boy?" he joked.

Zack fought the impulse to punch Sam right on the side of his fat head. He was such an easy target with his eyes shut.

Zack glanced over at Terry. Terry quietly mouthed the word *loser* and grinned. Zack smiled back.

"Sam!" Darla said crossly. She reached out a hand and whacked him on the head. Sam's eyes flew open.

Zack wanted to laugh out loud. He and Terry grinned at each other.

"Hey, chick!" Sam complained. He rolled over and slowly sat up.

"I'm not 'chick,' " Darla snapped. "And it's not nap

time. We've gotta work. And even though you are a lamebrain, you've got to help."

Darla narrowed her eyes at Sam. "Aren't you the one who was going hyper over the grade for this project? Something about being eligible for football?" she needled him.

Sam pressed his mouth together. "Yeah, yeah, yeah. So what?" He looked over at Zack. "Some of us can play football. Some of us..."

"Cut," Darla said. She frowned.

Darla was definitely all right. Darla sure could handle Sam.

Besides, it wasn't his style to *say* anything to get back at Sam. He was going to *do* something. What it would be, he didn't know yet. He scrunched up his face. But when he thought of it, it would be great.

"We have only a week left," Darla went on. "And our ideas aren't that great. Mrs. Ames wants really spectacular—EEEEEEEEEEK!" Darla screeched, jumping to her feet.

Jenaya followed. She jumped up and screeched too. "EEEEEEEEK! What was it?" she yelled at Darla.

Darla's face drained of color. "A mouse! I swear! It was a huge mouse!" She pointed at the open cupboard. "It went in there!"

Darla hopped up on a desk. Jenaya scrambled up on one too.

Zack looked over at the cupboard. Books were

stacked in neat rows. But there was plenty of room for a mouse—or even a rat—to slither in between them.

"EEEEEEK!" Darla repeated.

The door to the core area opened. Mrs. Ames poked her head around the corner.

Uh-oh, trouble, Zack thought. Was he going to get in trouble with his group?

"What *is* going on in here?" Mrs. Ames asked. "I asked for drama in your projects, but not disturbance." She looked at the five students.

"Mrs. Ames, there's a mouse in here!" Darla said. She pointed at the cupboard. "It went in there. Can you get the custodian to kill it?"

"I don't want to work in here," Jenaya complained. "I don't want to work with any mouse running around."

"Now, girls, relax," Mrs. Ames said. "We already have the custodian putting out poison for the mouse. We just haven't been able to catch him yet. The mouse is more afraid of you than you are of him.

"There's no more room in the classroom. The groups are all spread out. Just get back to work. You'll be fine."

Mrs. Ames shut the door. Zack looked at everyone.

Slowly, Darla sat down on top of the teacher's desk. She opened her notebook.

"Okay, fine," Darla said. "But I'm staying up here on this desk."

"Me too," Jenaya said. She crossed her legs on her desk top.

"I'm staying on the floor," Sam said. "I'm not afraid of some stupid little mouse. In fact," he went on, "me and my cousin like to trap 'em and blow 'em up with firecrackers tied to their tails. Rats too," he added. "It's cool. They blow sky high," he said, waving his arm in the air.

Sam was such a jerk. He's lying, Zack thought. Sure, maybe he did that to mice. But not rats. Zack knew there was no way to tie firecrackers to rats' tails without the chance of getting bitten. Sam's big mouth was at it again.

"That's not all. We do it to snakes too," Sam continued. "We trap and poison snakes and microwave 'em!" He grinned at the group. He sat down on a chair, tipped it back against the wall, and hooked his thumbs in his belt.

"Sick," Darla said. "Sam, you are really sick," she added, wrinkling her nose in disgust.

Sam just couldn't quit, could he? Zack thought in disgust. What a liar. There was no way for anyone to poison or trap snakes. No way at all. You had to have sticky board or glue board and hope they slithered onto it. Sam was bragging about things that weren't true.

"Hey, look at these," Sam said. His chair was next to some shelves. He leaned down and held up some dark, small objects. "They look like little footballs."

Zack almost exploded in laughter. Those weren't little footballs! He knew exactly what they were! Proof positive that Sam didn't know anything about rats. Oh, if

Sam only knew what he was holding...

"Eeeeeew!" Darla exclaimed. "Drop those, Sam. They look like mouse poop! They *are!*" She scooted herself away from the edge of the desk.

"You *are* sick, Sam!" Jenaya said loudly.

Terry looked at Zack. Together they began to laugh.

"Sam, good job," Terry said, gasping for air.

Zack held his sides. They almost hurt from laughing.

Sam looked mad. He had dropped the little brown objects when Darla yelled. He got up and began washing his hands at the sink. So much for Sam and his big-shot attitude, Zack thought, still grinning.

Then Zack looked carefully at the walls in the room. He was looking for a tell-tale sign. There! Over there, he could see a grease mark down low on the wall. That and the droppings had told the story.

There was no mouse in the core area at all. He knew exactly what it was. And somehow, he was going to get Sam back for all the Bug Boy stuff. And Sam's big mouth was going to help him do it. He just had to figure out a plan.

8
Plan for Murder!

The bell rang, marking the end of English class. Zack watched everyone leave.

"Hey, Zack," Terry called. He waited at the door of the classroom. "Aren't you coming to P.E.?" he asked.

"Uh, yeah," Zack said. He looked over at Mrs. Ames, who was talking to Jenaya. "I just gotta talk to Mrs. Ames for a second. Wait up, will you?" he asked.

"Sure." Terry raised a hand and opened the door. "I'll be outside," he said. "Hurry up."

Jenaya left. Mrs. Ames looked at Zack. He swallowed hard. This was the first part of his plan. He had thought of it in a burst of inspiration. Could he pull it off? he wondered.

Zack checked the classroom once more to make sure no one was there. He didn't want anyone to hear this.

"May I help you with something, Zack?" Mrs. Ames asked.

"Y-y-yes," Zack stammered. Why was it he couldn't talk to people he didn't know too well? He had to do this, though. It was part of his plan to get Sam. Come on, he argued with himself. Just do it.

Mrs. Ames smiled at him. "Well, what can I do for you?" she asked. She sat down at her desk and rested her chin on her hands.

Zack took a deep breath. "You—you know the mouse in the core area?" Zack asked.

Mrs. Ames frowned a little. "Yes." She sat up. "What about it?" she asked, puzzled.

"Well—well, it isn't a mouse in there. I know why the custodian hasn't been able to kill it," Zack said. He glanced nervously at the door again. He sure didn't want anyone overhearing *this* conversation.

"Why is that?" Mrs. Ames asked. She still looked puzzled. "How do you know?"

Zack colored above his collar. "My—my dad owns a pest control business," he said.

Mrs. Ames suddenly smiled. "Oh, yes. You're the one

who comes to school in the truck with the ant on it. The Squish 'Em Squad. It's a great idea! So catchy!" she added.

Maybe a hole could open up in the classroom floor and he could drop right in, Zack thought. Even his teachers knew he was the Bug Boy. Great idea—right.

"Anyway, it's a rat, not a mouse. I know it," Zack said.

He hoped Mrs. Ames wouldn't ask him how he knew. Because he wasn't going to tell her. No way! He couldn't talk to a lady teacher about the difference between mouse poop and rat poop. He went on quickly before Mrs. Ames could ask him.

"And the custodian is putting out little doses of D-Con. I can see the little bits of blue stuff. But they're not strong enough to do anything to a rat," Zack explained. He gestured with his hands. "The custodian needs to put out a single dose—a big one. Rats like to eat a lot in one place. Plus, she needs to put tracking powder near the walls and in the cupboards."

"Tracking powder? What does that do?" Mrs. Ames asked. She got up from her desk and walked over to Zack.

"It gets on the rat. Rats groom themselves. You know. Like a cat," Zack went on. "When a rat washes itself, the poison in the tracking powder kills it. You know. When it gets in its mouth. You can buy tracking powder at any hardware store, I think," Zack finished.

He shouldered his backpack. He adjusted the strap.

Then he looked at Mrs. Ames. She was standing there with her mouth slightly open.

"Well—thank you, Zack," she said slowly. "I'll tell Ms. Fogarty, the custodian."

"So, that's why the rat hasn't been caught," Zack said. "Not enough poison. But, Mrs. Ames," he said, "please don't tell anyone I told you. Not even Ms. Fogarty. Please?"

Zack held his breath, waiting. All he needed was to have Mrs. Ames announce to the class, "Guess what, class? Our own Bug Boy is going to help catch the rat!" He almost shuddered thinking about it. He could never face his classmates if that happened.

Mrs. Ames smiled. "Don't worry, Zack," she reassured him. "It'll be our little secret. I understand." She looked at the clock on the wall. "You'd better get to your next class. Would you like a tardy excuse?" she asked, reaching for a pad of paper on her desk.

"Hey, yeah, thanks," Zack said. "Oh, and one for Terry too. He's waiting for me."

"Of course," Mrs. Ames said. She wrote out two slips. She handed them to Zack. "Thanks again for your help," she said.

"No problem," Zack said. He took the notes. Yes! he thought. The first part of his plan was falling into place!

Quickly, he walked to the door. Terry was still outside.

"What were you doing?" Terry asked. "Reading her

an essay?" he joked.

"Naah," Zack said. "I had to ask her about the story," he fibbed. "I still don't really get it."

Terry was his friend. But Zack didn't want him to know about his plan. Not until it worked anyway.

"Me either," Terry said. "Maybe you can explain it to me."

Terry and Zack walked through the double doors at the end of the hall. The bright sunshine made Zack blink. Just a few students were still walking through the quad. It looked as if most kids were already in class.

"Looks like everyone's in class," Terry said. "Let's hurry." He broke into a jog. "I'm not getting detention for tardies one more time. My grandma'll kill me."

"I've got tardy excuses for us," Zack said. He grinned and waved the pink papers in the air.

Terry slowed down. He grinned back. "Good thinking," he said.

The boys walked up to the doors of the boys' locker room of the gym. They pushed the doors open.

"Tardies today, gentlemen?" Coach Dunwoody's voice barked at them from his office.

Zack and Terry stopped. Zack turned to see Coach's huge figure looming in the doorway. He froze in his tracks. His mouth felt dry. He couldn't say a word.

Silence. Coach looked at the two boys. Terry looked at Zack.

"Um, no, sir," Terry said quickly. "We were talking to

our English teacher." He grabbed the notes from Zack. He thrust them at Coach Dunwoody.

Coach took the notes and read them. Then the corners of his eyes crinkled a little in a smile. "Okay, you two clowns. Get going," he joked.

Whew, Zack thought. "Thanks," he muttered to Terry. They dropped their backpacks on the floor in front of their lockers.

"How come you didn't say anything?" Terry asked. He twirled the combination on his lock.

"I—I don't know," Zack said. He unsnapped his lock from the locker. He began taking off his shoes. "I hate talking in front of people. I kind of blank out."

"Oh," Terry grunted. "I don't like it either." He looked over at Zack. "So what are you gonna do for our presentation in English then?" he asked. He began pulling his shirt off over his head.

"I don't know," he said slowly. "I—I was thinking about staying home sick." He tossed his shoes into his locker. They thumped against the metal.

"And let *me* down?" Terry asked. He raised his eyebrows. "No way, man! If *I* have to be there, *you* have to be there too." He unzipped his backpack. He pulled out a pair of clean shorts and a shirt.

Great, Zack thought. He couldn't let Terry down. So far, Terry was his only friend at Paine Middle School. Zack felt a stab of panic.

9

The Body Is Discovered

Zack looked over at his dad in the truck seat beside him. He couldn't believe how quickly the week was going. Tuesday and Wednesday flew by. It was already Thursday. And on Monday, he'd have to make a presentation in English class. Zack felt a chill run down his spine. Time was moving too fast.

Helping his dad after school was hard work. And it seemed like the phone rang all the time at home. People really liked the ad in the Yellow Pages. Some people even said they had seen the truck driving around, and that was why they had called.

Zack was so busy. He almost felt like he didn't have time to be a kid.

The truck pulled up in front of the school. Here we go again, Zack told himself. Giant ant and all. The Squish 'Em Squad has arrived. He almost groaned aloud.

"Bye, Dad," he said quickly. He grabbed his backpack. He kept his head down as he opened the door and hopped out. Now if he could just make it to the building before anyone said anything dumb.

Did he hear little ripples of laughter follow him across the grass? Or was he imagining it? He gave a quick glance before he went inside.

Was that group of girls giggling at him? He sighed. When would this torture ever end?

English class finally arrived. Zack had been dreading it. They were just about finished planning the presentation. But their ideas weren't that great. Zack knew it. His whole group knew it. He dreaded their presentation. He worried that the class would laugh at him and his group.

Worse yet, Zack didn't have a part yet either. His stomach was in knots. He'd make a fool of himself. He just knew it.

"Okay. Let's meet with our groups," Mrs. Ames told the class. "You have only today and tomorrow to finish."

Desks clattered and students began talking loudly. Zack followed his group into the core area.

As soon as Zack walked in, he knew it. The rat. It was dead. The odor was faint, but he could smell it.

Zack looked around at the others. They couldn't tell. He saw it in their faces. They suspected nothing. His heart beat faster.

He looked at Sam and fought back a smile. You're just about to get yours, buddy, he thought sarcastically.

"Let's get started," Darla said. The group members pulled out their *Pathways to English* books.

Zack looked uneasy. "Uh—I forgot my book," he stammered.

"I'll get you one," Darla said. "There are some extras in that far cupboard."

Here we go, Zack thought. The rat must be lying dead on that side of the room—and probably in that very cupboard.

Zack crossed his fingers. He hoped everything would work as planned.

Darla stood up. She opened the cupboard.

"AAAAAAAAH! AAAAAAAAH! A dead something! It's huge!" Darla shrieked. She slammed the cupboard door shut. She ran into the main classroom, still screaming.

Zack hid a smile. He looked at Sam. Sam looked a

little green. Hah, he thought.

"What is it?" Terry asked. He walked to the cupboard. He looked inside.

Zack looked over at Sam again. Sam had backed into the classroom. He had his head down.

"Cool!" Terry said, looking at the rat. "Hey, man, check it out! This is one big rat!" He knelt down. He stared at it. "It kinda smells, though."

Zack walked over. He bent down and looked. It was a big one, all right. It was deader than dead too. Phew. It was just beginning to smell.

Zack could hear Darla yelling, "Get it out! Get it *out!* Please, Mrs. Ames!"

Kids from all the other classrooms had begun crowding at the windows, trying to peer through the closed blinds. Kids from Mrs. Ames' class pushed into the doorway. But no one came too close, except some of the guys.

In the doorway, Mrs. Ames sighed. "Ms. Fogarty is always busy somewhere in the school. I'll have to send someone to the office and say it's an emergency. With luck, she'll make it before too long." Mrs. Ames looked around at the students. "Who wants to go to the office?"

One of the girls raised her hand. "Yoshanda? Thanks, dear," Mrs. Ames said. "It sure would be nice if we could get rid of it right away." She sighed again and shook her head.

Loud talking and laughter filled the air as everyone

waited. Zack swallowed hard. Now he had to do it. Go for it, he told himself.

"Uh, Mrs. Ames?" he said. He stood up in front of the cupboard.

"Yes, Zack?" Mrs. Ames asked. She looked puzzled. Zack could tell she was probably wondering why he would want to call attention to himself. After all, he had begged her to be quiet about the rat. Hah, Zack thought. Just wait. He was going to put his plan into effect.

"Uh, Sam here always does stuff with rats and mice. He's not afraid of them." Zack tried to look as innocent as he could. He saw Sam's face drain of color. Gotcha, buddy, Zack almost snickered to himself.

"Yes? Go on?" Mrs. Ames said. She waited. She looked curious.

"I'm sure Sam wouldn't mind picking up the rat. He could just drop it in a plastic bag. Then he could take it to the custodian's office," Zack suggested. This was perfect. He fought the urge to laugh out loud.

Mrs. Ames looked relieved. She looked over at Sam. "Please, Sam. Would you?" she asked.

Yes! Zack wanted to shout and jump up and down. Now Sam really looked nervous. The color drained from his face.

Everyone grew quiet. All the faces turned toward Sam. They waited for Sam's answer.

"I—ah—I—" Sam's face was the face of a drowning man.

It's *your* turn to squirm, Zack jeered silently. He folded his arms and leaned back against the cupboard. He stared unblinkingly at Sam.

"I—ah—" Sam's face was stricken. "O—okay. But—but I don't want everybody looking over my shoulder. Just get everyone away from the doorway. Okay?" he asked Mrs. Ames. "I have to concentrate."

Huh! Zack knew why Sam didn't want witnesses. He didn't want anyone to see how afraid he was. Sam didn't have a clue about what to do with a dead rat.

Mrs. Ames looked surprised. Usually Sam looked for opportunities to show off in front of everybody. But not this time, Zack thought gleefully.

"Well, okay," she said. "All right, class," she said, raising her voice. "Get back to your places. Work on your story questions. We'll finish up in our groups as soon as Sam takes care of the rat."

Muttering and laughing, the students returned to their desks. Zack watched Sam stumble back into the core.

Terry looked at Zack. "What are you doin'?" he whispered, grinning.

"Guess!" Zack whispered back.

Sam walked closer to the cupboard. He wrinkled up his nose. He made a face. He shut his eyes. "It stinks. I think I'm gonna throw up," he whined.

He knelt down. He looked inside at the rat. The stiff body lay next to some books.

"Sick!" he said. He turned around. He looked

pleadingly at Zack. He took a deep breath. "Hey, buddy. Please help me out. Just this once?" he begged. "You do this all the time, right?"

"I thought you did too," Zack said. He began to smile. "What's the matter? It's not like the ones you blow up with firecrackers?"

"Please?" Sam asked. "I can't do this. I—I'll owe you one. Okay?" he asked. He stood up and looked at Zack.

Zack took a breath. He tightened his mouth. "You'll owe me more than *one* if I help you," he said. "I don't ever want to hear anything about Bug Boy again."

Zack saw Sam blink in surprise.

"And not only that. If you hear anyone *else* say anything like that, I want you to handle them," Zack finished. He stared at Sam. "Got that?"

"But..." Sam began.

"Come on, Terry," Zack said curtly. "Let's leave Sam with the rat. Since he knows what he's doing. I'm getting bored waiting for something to happen."

Zack turned to walk out of the core. Terry began to follow, grinning.

"Wait!" Sam begged. He frowned. "Okay. Deal. No more Bug Boy." He looked at Zack. "But don't you tell anyone you did this for me. All right?"

"No problem," Zack said. "I'll never say anything— unless you blow it about Bug Boy. Then," Zack pointed to Terry, "I've got a witness."

Terry grinned. He gave Zack the thumbs-up sign.

"There won't be anyone at school who won't know what really happened in here today." Zack stared at Sam cooly. He folded his arms again. "Any questions?"

Sam sighed. "No. Got it," he said reluctantly. He frowned.

"All right. Let's get rid of this thing," Zack said. He took a pair of rubber gloves from the box next to the sink. He pulled them on. He snapped a plastic bag out of a box and handed it to Terry.

Zack looked into the classroom. Everyone was busy working. Every now and then, someone would look up. But Mrs. Ames was right there to make everyone get back to work.

Zack knelt down. "You'd better get down here too, Sam," he said. "Unless you want people to know what a chicken you really are."

Sam made a face and knelt down next to Zack. But he turned his head away with a pained expression.

Zack grabbed the rat and dropped it into the bag. It made a small thud. Terry tied the neck of the bag shut. Yuck, Zack thought. He didn't like this either. But it was his job.

"Sick!" Sam said. He shuddered and jumped to his feet.

Zack tossed the gloves into the waste container. He looked at Sam and Terry

"Okay, amigos," he joked. "Let's send this rat to ratland, or wherever."

Terry gave the bag to Sam. Sam held it at arm's length. Together, the three walked out. The classroom erupted in noise.

"Did ya get it?"

"Eeeew! There it is!"

"Awesome!"

Sam left with the rat. Zack knew Sam was probably dying all the way to the custodian's office. Too bad for him!

"Awesome, man!" Terry gloated. "I can't believe you did it!" He and Zack high-fived each other.

What a day! He had done it. Zack hid a grin. Maybe this was the end of Bug Boy! It had to be! Maybe now he could have a life at Paine Middle School.

"Back to your groups, class," Mrs. Ames said.

Oh, no! Zack shut his eyes. In all the excitement, he had forgotten about the English presentation. But the memory came rushing back.

"I don't know if I want to come back in here," Darla said as their group walked into the core. She made a face and peered around the room, looking for extra rats. "Eeeew. It still smells in here."

"If we don't get going, we're dust," Jenaya reminded her. "Our presentation is so lame. I've heard about some of the others, and they're good. They're gonna laugh us out of town. We're doomed." She sank down on the floor. She rested her chin in her hands.

"And Zack," Darla said, looking right at him. Zack's stomach flipped. "You don't even have a part yet," she said, smoothing her skirt as she sat on a desk.

"Yeah, buddy," Terry chimed in. He grinned at Zack. "What are *you* going to say?" he teased.

Zack's stomach churned. The presentation. It was bad enough having to talk in front of the whole class. But if the presentation was dumb on top of it...

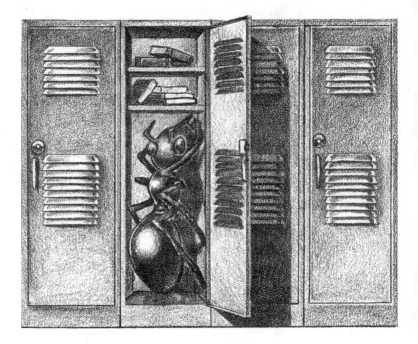

10

No More Bug Boy

"Dad!" Zack said as soon as he got into the truck after school. "Can you help me?"

Bill turned to look at Zack. "Sure, son. What is it?" he asked. He drove away from the school.

"Can—can my English group borrow the big ant from the top of the truck?" Zack asked. "We—uh—need it for our presentation." He held his breath. He watched his dad.

Bill started to laugh. "What?" he asked. He slapped the steering wheel in glee. The truck swerved. "You want to take the ant to class?" He laughed again, his eyes crinkling up.

"Hey! Dad! Watch where you're driving!" Zack exclaimed. His dad straightened out the wheel. The truck got into the right lane.

"I can't believe it," Bill said, still laughing. "You die every day when I drop you off at school."

Zack looked down at his hands. Oh, great. His dad was so proud of his business. And all along, he had known how Zack felt about the bug truck. Zack hadn't wanted him to know.

"You think I didn't notice?" Bill asked, looking at Zack's embarrassed face. "And now you want to take the ant *with* you? That beats everything! Wait till I tell your mother!" And he began to laugh again.

"Well? Can I? Please? I won't let anything happen to it," Zack begged. He watched his dad's face.

"Sure, son. Of course. But why on earth would you need the giant ant?" Bill asked.

During the rest of the afternoon, in between pest control calls, Zack explained. He told his dad the story of "If I Forget Thee, Oh Earth" and about the class projects. He finished just as they were pulling into the carport behind the apartment.

"And so, our group decided that there's a lot of scary stuff out now about bugs. You know—they get immune to sprays and stuff."

Zack and his dad locked up the truck. They began walking to the apartment. Zack turned to his dad.

"Plus a lot of antibiotics don't work any more the way they used to," Zack went on. "So I offered to bring the giant ant."

He actually couldn't believe he had suggested it. But the group had been desperate for good ideas. And Darla, Jenaya, Terry, and Sam had jumped on the idea. They thought it was awesome.

And in return, he didn't have to say much in front of the class. He just had to stand by the ant and say, "Oh my gosh, Zelda. We used too much bug spray!" He thought he might write it on a card and read it. He wouldn't even have to look at the class. He could just look at the ant.

Monday came too soon, even after a weekend of baby-sitting for screaming, hair-pulling, pony-stealing sisters. And the phone had practically rung off the hook. "Squish 'Em Squad, may I help you?" Zack could say it in his sleep.

Zack thought about their presentation. His stomach tightened. He couldn't believe he was actually going to do this. The Bug Boy was going to take the giant ant to school. He must be crazy.

Everyone in the group said Mrs. Ames would like it. They all said that was the kind of goofy stuff she liked. It should help his grade, which wouldn't hurt since he never said anything in class.

Best of all, he remembered what Darla had said. "Zack! That's a wonderful idea!" Her eyes had sparkled. He felt kind of funny when he thought about that.

The school loomed ahead. Zack saw dozens of kids milling about. A big knot formed in his stomach. What was he doing? But it was too late to back out now. His group was counting on him.

Zack's dad drove around to the side of the school. The entrance to the English class was close by. No one was around.

Together, Zack and his dad unfastened the giant ant from the top of the truck. Zack lugged it into the building and up the stairs. A couple of kids saw him and cracked up.

"Cool! What are you using that for?" one asked.

"English," Zack muttered. He knew his face was as red as the ant.

All day, Zack expected to hear jokes about the giant ant in the core area. But no one said anything, except Darla and Terry.

"Did you bring it?" Darla asked excitedly. "Is it here?"

"Yeah," Zack mumbled. He felt his face get warm.

"That's great, Zack!" she said, smiling. "I know we're going to get a good grade!"

"The ant's here? You're all right, man," Terry said. He high-fived Zack. "No one'll ever call *you* a chicken!" he said. Then he flapped his arms like a chicken and squawked, grinning. "Not like *some* people we know!" he said, looking over at Sam.

Sam hadn't said a word about the ant. Sam hadn't said anything about Bug Boy since the day of the rat discovery. He had even given Andrew a hard look in science class when Andrew said something about it. But Zack knew he'd have to watch him anyway.

The bell finally rang for English class. Zack walked in with Terry. He felt a little sick. Was he really going to go through with this? Through the doorway into the core, he could see the giant ant. Kids crowded in the doorway, pointing and talking about it.

"Hey! Isn't that the Squish 'Em Squad's giant ant?"

"What's it doing in there?"

"Why is it here?"

Darla got the group together before the bell. "Look," she said. "I think we should ask to go first."

"First?" Zack's voice almost squeaked. No way! He wanted to put this off as long as he could.

"Yes, first," Darla said. "I know teachers. You always get a better grade if you go first. Besides, then it's over. We can just cruise the rest of the time, watching the other groups," she finished, smiling.

"Sounds fine to me," Terry said. "How about it, Zack?" he asked, looking at Zack.

"Yeah," Zack sighed. He might as well get it over with. Darla was right. He couldn't feel any worse than he did right now.

"Sure!" Jenaya said. She looked excited.

Sam just grunted. Sam could hardly look at his group since the rat episode. Served him right.

Before he knew it, his group was in front of the class. Everyone sat up in their desks, grinning. The giant ant stood in front of the room, grinning back.

The group began. Everyone said his or her lines. Darla and Jenaya had memorized theirs.

Finally, Zack mumbled his line. He read from a card he had printed carefully.

"Oh my gosh, Zelda. We used too much bug spray!" he choked out. He kept his head down. He just looked at the ant and not the class. That helped.

Everyone in the class laughed. Some people even started clapping after his line. He didn't think it was *that* funny.

Finally, it was over. Zack dragged the giant ant back into the core with Terry.

The class kept clapping and clapping and laughing.

"Awesome!"

"How did you guys think of that?"

"That was great!"

"Absolutely wonderful, group," Mrs. Ames said. She smiled broadly. Zack saw her write some notes. He hoped they were good.

Darla smiled at him. He grinned back. Whew, he thought, sinking down into his desk. At least that was over. He'd get the ant after P.E. class, when school was over.

"See you tomorrow," Terry called after P.E. class. "Need help with the ant?" he asked.

"Nah, that's okay. I can handle it," Zack said. "My dad's meeting me at the side entrance again. See you tomorrow," he finished.

Zack lugged the giant ant down the stairs again and outside. He sat next to the ant on the grass, waiting for his dad. A few kids walked by.

"Hey, I heard you guys did something pretty good in English class with that," one girl said with a smile.

Zack smiled back. It hadn't been that bad, after all.

His dad pulled up in the bright yellow truck. "Squish 'Em Squad," the red letters almost shouted.

"How did it go, Zack?" his dad asked. Together, they hoisted the ant back on top of the truck.

"It went okay, Dad. No," Zack said, "it was great, actually. Thanks for letting us use the ant." They fastened the ant back on. Both of them climbed into the truck.

"Well, son, I've got some good news," Bill said. "I've been really busy the last two weeks. We're growing really fast." He started the engine. "Almost too fast for just one man to handle. The bank thinks so too.

"Today I had a meeting at the bank," Bill continued. "I showed them my receipts from the last two weeks. They're going to lend me a little money to pay someone part-time to work afternoons and weekends." Bill steered the truck away from the curb. He pulled into traffic.

"What?" Zack almost shouted. He looked at his dad.

Could he believe what he was hearing?

"Yup." His dad smiled at him. "So as soon as I can hire someone, you're free to go out for spring football. If you're still interested.

"You really helped when I needed it," his dad said smiling. "That made the difference. Because of your help, I didn't have to turn down any calls. And you helped your mother too. You worked like a Washington and made us proud." His dad braked for a red light.

"And it shouldn't take me long to find someone," his dad continued. "I got some good leads from the people at the bank."

"Yes!" Zack exclaimed. "Thanks, Dad!"

"Of course, we'll still need your help once in a while," Bill added. "But you should still have plenty of time for football and friends."

Zack sat up straight. He couldn't believe it! Time for football. Time for friends. No more bug calls.

And Zack knew exactly what to say if anyone ever teased him again about being Bug Boy. He'd just grin at them and say—"Don't bug me!"